KIDWORMS

Written by Johanne Mercier
Translated by Daniel Hahn
Illustrated by Clare Elsom

PHOENIX YARD BOOKS

More stories with Arthur

CONTENTS

For Alain F.

JM

For Jesse

DH

For Paul

CE

Chapter 1
My new Job

I'm Arthur and I'm seven, and starting tomorrow I've got a new job. I'm going to sell earthworms. I started getting interested in worms because of my duck. He lives at my grandparents' house and worms are his favourite food. When I really want to give him a treat, we go worm-hunting together. Last Sunday, that's what we did. And because it was a rainy day, and because the day before was a rainy day, we found loads and loads of them.

When Grandad saw me arrive with a huge bucket full of worms, he had an idea.

"You should sell them at the side of the road, Arthur."

"But no one will want to buy worms. Not everyone has a duck."

"Everyone who goes fishing in Picket Lake will be rushing to buy them from you, lad. The only problem…"

Grandad leaned in towards me. He looked left and he looked right, and then whispered:

"The only problem is your grandmother."

"Why?"

"She doesn't like earthworms all that much."

"That isn't a very big problem. I won't be selling them to her."

"The problem is, you've got to store them in the fridge, Arthur. You see, they have to be kept cool."

"In the fridge?"

"You've got to. Before I go fishing, I always manage to hide my worms in the fridge."

"And Grandma's never found them?"

"Never! Your grandfather is a cunning old thing."

As Grandma was coming towards us, Grandad and I started talking about something else.

"What are the two of you plotting now?" asked Grandma when she saw my bucket full of earth.

"Nothing" Grandad and I replied at once.

"Let me guess. You're going to sell earthworms."

I answered, "yes", and that I was going to sell millions, and I was going to be very rich, and, with the money I'd make, I'd buy her a present, and that it was going to be a jewel.

Grandma laughed.

"You're very kind, young Arthur," she said, heading back towards the house.

But just before she went back in she threw me a warning look and added:

"But you're absolutely not putting those dirty worms of yours in the fridge, Arthur. You understand? You're not going to do what your grandfather does!"

Grandad gave a funny smile.

Chapter 2
Here We go!

My grandma is really very nice. Even though she doesn't like earthworms all that much, she still helped me with my new job. She brought out a little table and a chair, and she wrote

"WORMS FOR SalE"

on a piece of cardboard. But when we tried to stand it up in front of the table, it kept getting blown away. So we gave up on the idea of having a sign.

Grandma put a jug of water, a glass and a cupcake on my table. She wished me luck and went to sit on the front porch with Grandad. As for me, I stayed at my table, all on my own, by the side of the road, with my duck… and my earthworms.

I waited.

I ate my little cupcake.

And I waited some more.

The problem was not that people weren't interested in earthworms. The problem was that almost no one ever came past on the little road outside my grandparents' house.

When the first car stopped right in front of my table, my heart almost burst, I was so nervous. From the porch, I heard Grandad shout.

"Your first customers, Arthur! Go for it, lad!"

I took a deep breath.

A lady got out of the car. She walked over to me. I said:

"Good morning. How many would you like?"

"One large and one small, please, young man."

"The big ones are 7p, the little ones are 5p."

The lady laughed. She said that wasn't very expensive, and that I could easily sell them for 50p. I replied that I agreed. I stuck my hand into the bucket. I dug around a little and pulled out the first earthworm. I was very happy, because it was a really long one.

"Aargh! How disgusting!" screamed the woman. "How horrible!"

I could hear Grandad laughing on the porch.

The lady walked back to her car, telling the boy who was waiting for her that I wasn't selling lemonade, only disgusting, germ-ridden bugs. The boy got out, slamming the door. He didn't look happy at all.

"I'm thirsty!" he shouted, walking towards my table.

"Darling, get back in the car at once!" the lady shouted.

The boy didn't listen to his mum. He stared right at me. Then he said something really awful:

"I want the duck!"

"What?" the lady asked.

"Buy me the duck!"

The lady looked at my duck, who was having a little stroll along the grass and pretending he hadn't heard a thing.

"How much for the duck?" asked the lady, sighing.

"He's not for sale!"

"I want the duck!" the boy yelled again.

"This duck's mine. I don't want to sell him, or give him away, or lend him to anyone or anything."

The boy made a terrible fuss. He said that he had dreamed of having a duck his whole life,

and that this was the exact one he wanted, and he wasn't leaving without it. And then he started to cry, even though it was only pretend crying.

"How much do you want for that wretched duck?" the lady asked me. "Ten pounds? Twenty? Fifty? A hundred?"

I shouted as loudly as I could:

"GRANDAD, COME QUICKLY!"

My grandfather came down from the porch. He whispered something in the lady's ear and the car shot off in a huge cloud of dust.

At the end of the day, I made a big decision. I announced to my grandfather, "I've given up my new job!"

Waiting by the side of the road, without selling anything, wasn't much fun. And besides, I'd almost lost my duck, and I didn't want to go through that again.

Grandad replied that you should never give up on things in life, not even when they're difficult. He added that he was sure I'd sell lots of worms tomorrow.

I asked, "How do you know?"

"He said he just knew. That was all."

Chapter 3
A magical Day

The next morning, Grandma made me pancakes before I set off for work. I settled down at my table and a car appeared. I was so disappointed when I saw it was just Cousin Eugene.

"Hello, Eugene!" called Grandad. "What a lovely surprise! Have you seen what Arthur's doing?"

"I'm selling earthworms!"

"Are you now?" said our cousin, without even looking at me.

"Eugene? Won't you give the boy some encouragement?" asked Grandad.

"Uh… yes. Jolly good, Arthur! Well done!"

"You'll buy some, won't you, Eugene?"

"Well, the thing is, personally, I'm really not all that keen on the earthworm species…"

My grandfather glared at him, so Eugene added, "Still, it's always useful having a few handy. I'll buy one from you, Arthur."

Grandad glared at him even harder, so

Eugene said, "I'll take a dozen! You can never be too well prepared."

I was really happy.

Cousin Eugene gave me a pound and I put his twelve worms in a box. He didn't even want his change. The sad thing was, when he went home he left his worms behind, on the table. Really absent-minded, our cousin.

A bit later, another car pulled up.

The one after that stopped, too. Then another… and another. That morning, everyone was driving down the little road. Everyone knew my grandfather, and everyone needed earthworms. It was a magical morning. Grandad helped me with the pennies, and the two of us had a real laugh together.

After lunch, Grandad suggested that I should have a bit of a rest, but I wasn't tired at all. I stayed at my table, even though I had hardly any worms left to sell.

Grandad did take a nap, sitting in the rocking chair on the porch, which was a real shame, because he didn't see the red truck that pulled up right in front of my table. And he didn't see the man with a moustache who called out to me:

"Are you selling worms, young man?"

"Yes, sir."

"I'll take four hundred and fifty!"

"How many?"

He said it again.

"Four hundred and fifty."

Each time I asked him how many he wanted, he always answered: "Four hundred and fifty."

I told him I could give him his four hundred and fifty earthworms... but not until the next morning. I ran over to Grandad to give him the good news.

Chapter 4
Top Secret

Grandad was right: four hundred and fifty earthworms are a lot! Especially when the sun's shining, and there isn't a single cloud in the sky.

What earthworms like is damp. So my grandfather and I decided to make some. We watered the patch of ground behind the house, the front lawn, down the sides, everywhere. And we managed to find thirty-seven earthworms in total.

"Only thirty-seven?" Grandad said.

"Are you sure you counted them right, Arthur?"

"Thirty-six now."

"Why thirty-six?"

"Oops... thirty-five."

"That's enough!" growled Grandad. "We've got to put that duck in the house! He's eating all our worms! We'll never get there at this rate!"

He grabbed hold of my duck and walked over to the house, scolding him as he went. He opened the door and put him down in the living room.

When my grandfather came back, my duck was following him. Grandma had put him out because she didn't like him being in the house when she was doing the hoovering.

I asked Grandad, "So how much money am I going to get for the worms?"

"About thirty pounds."

"What will I be able to buy?"

Grandad sighed.

"Arthur lad, I'm not sure we're going to manage to find four hundred and fifty earthworms."

"We will. We'll do it."

"It's a very big order."

"You always tell me I should never give up."

"I say that?"

Grandad had a little think.

"You're right, Arthur! We're going to try. But we're going to have to work hard tonight."

I was happy to work, even at night. I never really liked going to bed and doing nothing, anyway.

"Right, Arthur, I'm going to explain my secret plan."

"Why is it secret?"

"If your grandmother catches us hunting

for earthworms in the middle of the night, we're done for. Understand?"

I went to bed very early. That was the first part of the secret plan. I pretended to be asleep and then, later, Grandad gave the signal: three little taps on the wall. I climbed out of the bedroom window.

Grandad and I set to work. I watered the ground and Grandad looked for the worms. I put them into boxes and then tiptoed over to the house, to put them in the fridge. Grandma was asleep in the little bedroom at the back. The secret plan was working brilliantly.

But I ruined everything!

Trying to clear a bit of space for the worms in the fridge, I dropped a pot of jam on the floor. The noise echoed all the way through the house. I was about to escape when the kitchen light came on. And it didn't come on all by itself.

"Arthur?" asked Grandma.

"Yes?"

"What are you doing up?"

"I… I was… I…"

I was done for.

Chapter 5
A Night-time Mission

Grandad and I explained everything to Grandma: the order for four hundred and fifty earthworms; the man with the moustache; all of it. She gave us a funny look. Then she went back to her bedroom, and came back out in her dressing gown and her wellies.

"Grandma, what are you…?"

"You need a system, Arthur! We haven't a minute to lose. I'll water with the hose.

You hold the big torch. Geoffrey, you collect the worms. Put fifty in each box; it'll be easier to count them that way. What time tomorrow morning is this man coming to collect them?"

"At six."

"And you've already collected how many?"

"Fifty-two."

"Not great," said Grandma, grabbing the telephone. "I'm calling Eugene. He'll come over and give us a hand."

Cousin Eugene agreed. He asked his neighbour to help, and his neighbour woke up his son so that he could come, too. And everyone got to work. Grandma was the big boss, directing the whole operation.

"Arthur, some light here! Geoffrey, you dig over there. Eugene… Eugene, what on earth are you doing?"

"I'm keeping an eye on the duck, Aunt Margaret. He's trying to eat everthing."

"Get to work, Eugene! Dig!"

At two o'clock in the morning, we had five big boxes full of worms, but it still wasn't enough.

"If you ask me," said Cousin Eugene, yawning, "there isn't a single worm left anywhere round here."

"That's what I think, too," added Grandad, wiping his muddy hands on his trousers.

"Goodnight, everyone," said Eugene's neighbour.

"Goodnight," his son repeated like a zombie.

"Tsk, tsk!" said Grandma. "There may be no worms left here, but there are definitely some at the Harveys' place!"

So we raided the Harveys' garden, then the Hudsons', and Mrs Potter's place, too.

And we did it!

Chapter 6
The Delivery

At six o'clock on the dot, the man with the moustache appeared. I was waiting by the side of the road with Grandad and the four hundred and fifty earthworms. Proudly, I showed him my boxes.

The man sighed.

"Is there a problem?" Grandad asked.

"It's just that... the fishing trip's been cancelled. I don't really need worms anymore."

It was, without a doubt, the worst news I'd

ever heard in my whole life. Grandad and I nearly started crying, but the man put his hand in his pocket.

"Here you go, young man," he said, giving me thirty pounds to pay for the worms he wasn't buying.

He thanked us, and drove off.

"What are we going to do with four hundred and fifty earthworms?" muttered Grandad. "If your grandmother ever finds out that we've still got the worms, we're…"

"I think I might have an idea!"

And that morning, Grandad and I gave my duck the biggest treat ever.

More escapades with
Arthur coming soon

Arthur and the Yeti

Arthur and the Guard Dog

ARTHUR

AND THE **MYSTERY** OF THE EGG

JOHANNE MERCIER

ARTHUR

Johanne Mercier

It all started when this lady called Johanne thought about me in her head. Grandma said Johanne had written fifty-eight stories for children, and that one of her stories was made into a film. Grandma also said Johanne understands children because she used to be a teacher. But now she writes all day.

I think it must be really fun to write stories all day. When I grow up, I want to write stories like Johanne Mercier and I also want to be a pilot. Grandad says there's nothing to stop me doing both, but I think that writing stories and flying a plane at the same time is not a good idea.

Daniel Hahn

Daniel Hahn translated the stories. He took my French words, and wrote them in English. He said it was quite a difficult job, but Cousin Eugene said he could have done it much better, only he was busy that day. So we got Daniel to do it, as he's translated loads and loads of books before. He also said he wrote the words for a book called *Happiness is a Watermelon on your Head*, but everyone else said that book was just plain silly.

Daniel is almost as clever as Cousin Eugene and he lives in England in a house by the sea with a lot of books.

Clare Elsom

I was so happy when we met Clare Elsom. She got out her pencils and pens and scribbled until the scribbles looked just like me! Grandma and Grandad said the resemblance was uncanny.

Clare has so many pencils and pens – at least twenty of them – and she spends all day drawing in lots of different books. I'm not sure that you are allowed to draw in books, but she seems to get away with it.

I like Clare because she likes egg on toast and exploring new places and drawing me. But I think she wants my pet duck, so I will have to keep an eye on her.

Arthur and the Earthworms

ISBN: 978-1-907912-17-7

First published in French in under the title *Athur et les vers de terre* by Dominique et compagnie, a division of Les Éditions Héritage, Saint-Lambert,Canada. This edition published in the UK by Phoenix Yard Books Ltd, 2013.

Phoenix Yard Books
Phoenix Yard
65 King's Cross Road
London
WC1X 9LW
www.phoenixyardbooks.com

1 3 5 7 9 10 8 6 4 2
A CIP catalogue record for this book is available from the British Library
Printed in Great Britain